D0193316
Wallace & Gromit
in
Nick Park's
A CLOSE SHAVE
BBC BOOKS

It had been a hard day and Wallace was already fast asleep in bed. Gromit was also in bed but he was wide awake; he'd been knitting and drinking cocoa for ages, but still didn't feel at all tired.

And then he heard the lorry. It must, he thought, be a very large one indeed as the whole house began to vibrate, sending his ball of wool bouncing off the bedside table and across the floor. Gromit watched the lorry's headlights pass across his curtains, heard a squeal of brakes and knew that it must be stopping – only just in time – at the traffic lights in front of the house.

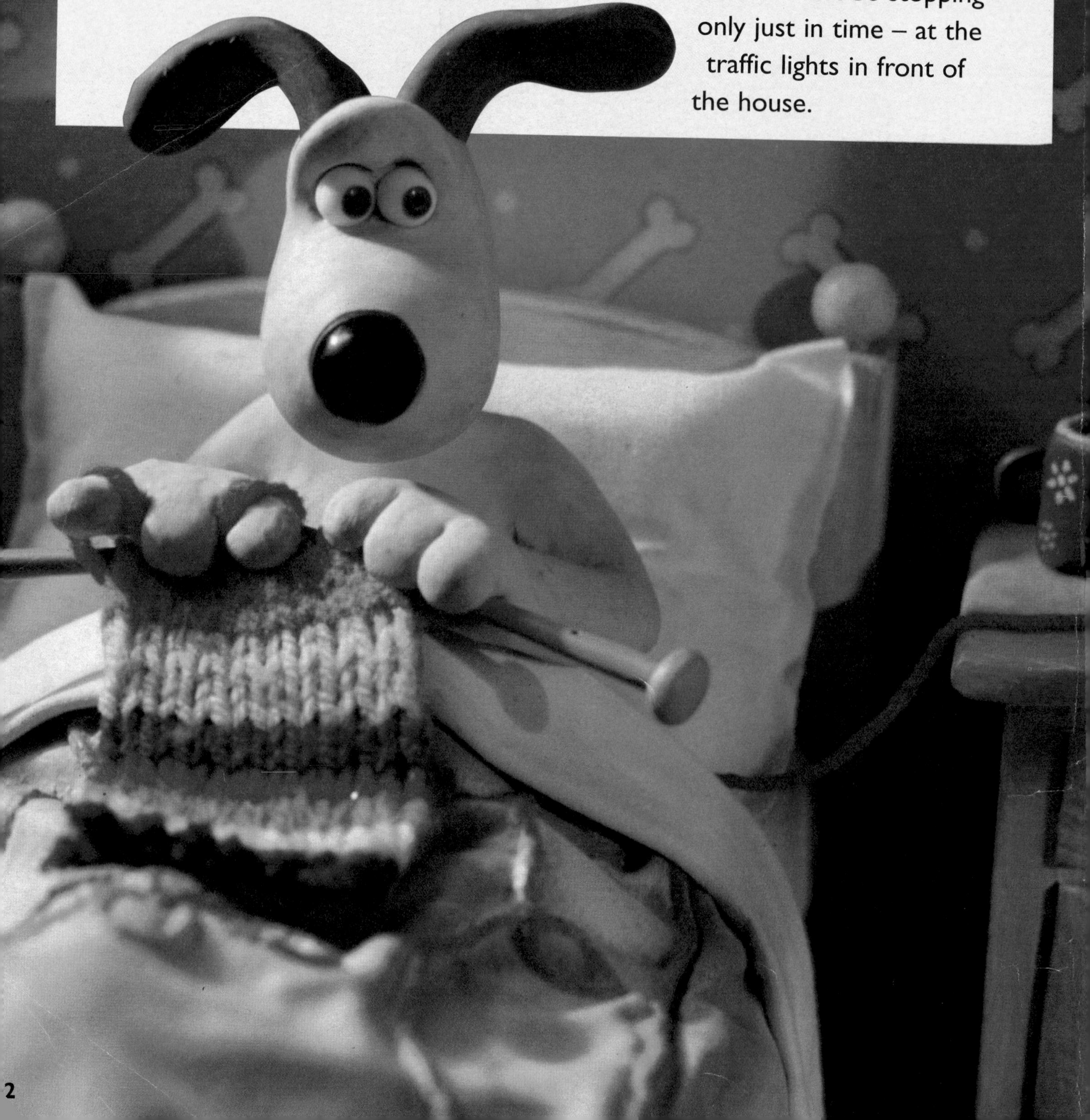

Outside in the cold night something very strange was happening. Something was desperately trying to escape through a gap in the side of the lorry. If Gromit had been watching he'd have seen two black legs, followed by a small white furry head, poke through the gap; he'd then have seen a lamb jump out and run off down the street.

Gromit wasn't watching, but the lorry driver was. In his wing-mirror he saw the whole incident, and as he started to open his door a woman's hand stopped him: 'No!' she said, and he closed it again. The driver sat and observed the lamb disappear through the garden gate of Number 62 West Wallaby Street – above it was a sign which said WALLACE AND GROMIT'S WASH'N'GO WINDOW CLEANING SERVICE.

As the lights changed, the driver, who was wearing a thick studded collar, made a quick note of the number and sped away.

Even though he'd gone to bed late, Gromit was, as usual, up first the next morning and was enjoying a nice cup of tea as he read a story about sheep rustling in the morning paper. A buzz from upstairs told him that Wallace was awake.

'Porridge today, Gromit!' Wallace called out. 'It's Tuesday!'

Gromit pulled a lever beside him and heard Wallace yell 'Geronimo!' as he was hurled through the hole in the floor, into his trousers and on to his chair. Pausing for the Auto-dresser to finish dressing Wallace, Gromit fired the porridge cannon, and – PFUMPF! – a dollop of the finest rolled oats landed squarely in Wallace's bowl.

Wallace smiled, but the smile was wiped off his face as the porridge cannon carried on firing

PFUMPF! PFUMPF! PFUMPF!

and he caught a dollop in his face. 'Turn it off!' he mumbled as

PFUMPF!

another load hit him.

Having discovered that the off switch on the porridge cannon didn't work, Gromit looked down and saw the wiring had been chewed through.

'Er... mice d'you think?' said Wallace.

A sound made Gromit look over his shoulder. There was nothing there. Leaving Wallace to clean up, he went off to investigate, and discovered a leaf on the rubber plant in the hall had been eaten.

'Well, I'll be,' Wallace called from the kitchen, 'have you been peckish during the night, Gromit? Someone's been at me cheese!'

Something decidedly odd was going on, thought Gromit.

'D'you think we should call in the pest control people?' he heard Wallace ask. Looking back into the sitting room, Gromit saw him in his armchair, feet up and staring at the newspaper – which had a large hole eaten out of it. And then the phone rang.

Wallace picked up the receiver and put on the loudspeaker. 'Hello, Wallace and Gromit's Wash'n'Go Window Cleaning Service! May we be of assistance?'

'Yes,' Gromit heard a slightly nervous voice reply. 'My windows need a jolly good clean... the wool shop in the High Street... soon as you can!'

'On our way, madam!' said Wallace, giving Gromit the thumbs-up.

Ever-efficient, Gromit had already pulled the lever down. This sent Wallace, in his armchair, shooting up through a hole in the ceiling and into the arms of an ingenious machine. In a matter of seconds, Wallace was manoeuvred into his crash-helmet, overalls and wellingtons and was finally lowered on to his motorbike. Moments later the two friends were roaring off down the road on their way to the High Street.

Meanwhile back at Number 62 a small woolly lamb continued to munch away at anything he could find to eat...

Roaring down the road, Gromit spotted a sign saying *Wendolene's Wools* and he unhitched the ladder from the sidecar. Exactly on time he stuck the ladder into a drain and pole-vaulted up the building; Wallace braked hard and came to a stop opposite the shop's front door.

Up above, Gromit came face to face with a very stern-looking dog wearing a thick studded collar. Unknown to Gromit, this was the driver of the lorry he'd heard screeching to a halt the night before. The dog glared at him and moved away. Wondering what he'd done wrong, Gromit attached a bungee cord to the shop's sign, jumped off the ladder and arrived just in time to collect the bucket and sponge Wallace had ready for him.

After handing the cleaning equipment over, Wallace looked up to see a lady waving at him from inside the shop.

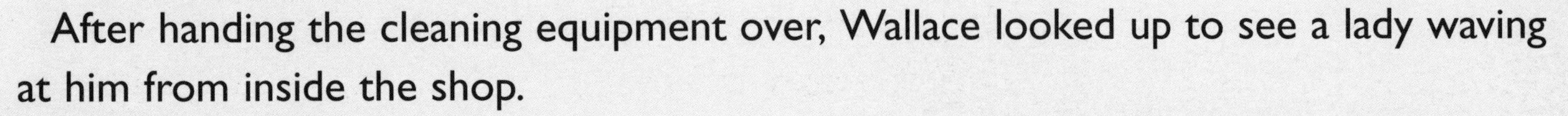

Completely forgetting that he should be helping Gromit, Wallace made for the door, muttering, 'Need wool, don't you lad?' as Gromit bounced down for his squee-gee.

'Thank you for coming so quickly,' said the lady, as he entered the shop.

Wallace didn't know what to do next, so he picked up a ball of wool from the bottom of the pile next to him. The pile promptly collapsed on to the floor.

'Oh, dear!' exclaimed Wallace, as the wool went everywhere. 'I'm so sorry.'

It was then that he saw a dog standing in the corner, looking at him as if he was a complete idiot, watching a ball of wool roll towards him.

'This is Preston,' said the lady, 'my dog.'

'All right, pooch?' said Wallace, going over and patting Preston on the head.

At the bottom of each bungee bounce, Gromit caught sight of what was happening in the shop. He saw Wallace and the wool shop owner picking up some wool, watched by that grim dog from upstairs, and on the next bungee bounce he was shocked to see them holding hands!

'What was it you wanted?' she said. Wallace blushed as Preston left the shop. 'My name's Ramsbottom, Wendolene Ramsbottom.'

'Charming,' Wallace grinned stupidly. 'I'm Wallace – the windows,' he said, dropping her hand when he realised he was still holding it. 'Is this place yours?'

'My father left it to me,' said Wendolene, nodding to a picture on the wall, 'along with his debts and a few other things. He was an inventor.'

'Well, I never!' said Wallace. 'I do a bit of that myself!'

'Oh,' said Wendolene, looking past him at Gromit, whose bounce had all gone and was now hanging upside down outside the shop. 'Your dog's waiting...'

Wallace and Gromit made their way back home, but Preston had already got there before them and he was sniffing around the back door. He had just found a small piece of wool caught in the dog-flap when he heard the sound of a motorbike. Seconds later he had hidden himself in the coal cellar.

When the two friends walked in the front door they found the house in a state of absolute chaos. Everything that could be chewed had been chewed.

'Good grief!' exclaimed Wallace. 'What's all this – burglars? Thieves? What a mess!'

Gromit, ears up, padded off towards the kitchen to investigate, where he found a small lamb stuck in a large pool of spilt treacle.

'Heavens above, Gromit!' said Wallace, coming in through the door. 'Look at this – the little chap must be really hungry. Come over here, lad, no need to be sheepish – we'll have to get you cleaned up.'

Down in the basement sat Wallace's pride and joy – the Knit-o-matic machine.
Wallace put the lamb into the washing tub. 'There,' he said, 'just a quick shampoo, nothing to fret over – we've tested it on Gromit, haven't we lad?'
Gromit frowned and slunk over to the control panel, set it to *Wash* and watched as the Knit-o-matic covered the lamb in suds.
Through a grille set in the floor, Preston's beady eyes watched what was going on with great interest, particularly when things started to go wrong.

Instead of a shampoo, the machine switched itself to *Light Shave* and sucked the lamb out of the tub, into *Auto-dry* and on down to the shaving unit.
'Oh, dear! Do something! Turn it off, Gromit!' shouted Wallace.
'Uh-oh, too late now!'

The Knit-o-matic seemed to have a life of its own: it clanked, it whirred, pulleys pulled and needles knitted. Seconds later, out came a small but perfectly formed woolly jumper, which the machine gently placed on Wallace's head.

'Brilliant, Gromit. Smashing, this,' said Wallace. 'Just a bit tight here and there.' Gromit looked from the jumper over to the Knit-o-matic's exit hatch where an even smaller lamb, shivering from the lack of wool, was coming out.

Wallace grinned and picked the lamb up. 'I think we'll call him Shaun, eh?'

Wallace made his way back upstairs with Shaun. There was, thought Gromit, something amiss down in the basement, but he couldn't work out what it was. He shut the door behind him.

In the gloom the metal grille in the floor creaked and swung open as Preston came up from the coal cellar. He looked with great interest at the Knit-o-matic until he spotted Wallace's drawing board. On it were the plans for the incredibly complex machine. Preston looked furtively left and right, quickly rolled them up and made his escape.

After breakfast the next morning, Gromit was leafing through the newspaper, trying to stop Shaun eating it and noting the headline story about a killer dog on the loose. The lamb was now wearing the jumper the Knit-o-matic had made from his very own wool, and lovely and snug it was too.

'You know we're doing the Town Hall clock tomorrow, Gromit,' said Wallace as he repaired the porridge cannon. Gromit looked daggers at him over the newspaper; knowing Wallace as he did, this could only mean trouble. Indeed, Wallace had great plans about adapting the cannon so that it could shoot soap suds and he was already adjusting it to fit the motorbike sidecar.

The following day, thinking Gromit would be too busy cleaning the Town Hall clock to notice, Wallace slipped off to visit the wool shop across the road. But Gromit did notice and he also spotted Wendolene's dog observing everything from a window above the wool shop. Moving his ladder, Gromit watched Wallace and Wendolene chatting away in the shop; he could hear Wallace explaining that window cleaning was just a temporary thing: inventing, that was what he really liked doing.

And then Gromit heard a lamb baaa-ing above him. Looking up he saw Shaun's head sticking out of a hole in the wall, and then it suddenly disappeared, as if yanked back by someone. Gromit climbed up the ladder and poked his head through the hole: yes, there was Shaun!

SSS-KAPPPOWW!

A violent flash exploded in front of Gromit. For a split second he thought he saw someone with a camera, but the light was so shockingly bright that he shot backwards, his head almost popping out of the hole.

What he couldn't have known was that the picture that had just been taken showed him as, of all things, a butchering *sheep killer*...

Sliding down the ladder, Gromit rushed straight into the wool shop. He completely ignored Wallace and Wendolene, who were still trying to have a sensible conversation, and went upstairs in search of the practical joker who had nearly blinded him.

Opening the first door he came to, Gromit went into the darkened room. It was totally empty, except for a family portrait on the wall of a jolly butcher with an axe. Walking in, Gromit accidentally kicked something on the floor. He looked down and saw a can of dog food labelled *Preston's Dog Food*.

As Gromit looked at the portrait, the jolly butcher's face fell away to reveal the very hole in the wall that he had peered through! Gromit didn't yet know it, but he had been set up...

Suddenly, he heard the noise of plaintive baaa-ing. Looking out of a window on to the back yard of the shop, Gromit saw a large lorry about to drive away. Odd, for a small wool shop, he thought – and then he saw Shaun's head poking through a gap in the side!

Pounding down the stairs, Gromit caught Wallace mumbling, 'What I'm trying to say – in a manner of speaking – is... um...' He scooted out of the back door just in time to undo the lorry's tailgate and release the grateful flock of sheep trapped inside.

In his rear-view mirror Preston watched the sheep thunder past Gromit. Just like a woolly tidal wave, they swept into the shop as Wallace took Wendolene's hand and said: 'Of all the women I've met – ahem, *ladies* – I've met – *you*...'

Then, at the crucial moment, the unstoppable flock took Wallace with them as they streamed out into the High Street. All he could do was wave and suggest he came back next week.

As the bleating, baaa-ing stampede disappeared, Gromit suddenly caught sight of Shaun. He was still inside the lorry and he couldn't get out because he was tied up. Gromit ran up the ramp and began undoing the rope. He was concentrating so hard on what he was doing he didn't hear the lorry's tailgate closing. The moment Shaun was loose he made a dash for freedom – but Gromit was too slow and the tailgate slammed shut.

Preston started the engine.

Gromit suddenly found the tables had been turned. He was now on the inside, looking out at Shaun! As the lorry moved away, all the little lamb could do was watch.

The next day, Wallace decided, was the worst of his whole life. The house was full to the brim with sheep which were eating anything, and to top it all Gromit had been arrested for killing a sheep! There was even a picture of him in the paper wielding an axe above a lamb's head.

'Caught bang to rights you were,' sighed Wallace. 'You really let us down this time, lad.'

Two sheep were munching on his newspaper, another was finishing off a packet of cream crackers (including the wrapper) and, as Wallace got up to answer the doorbell, a third slurped his cup of tea.

'Hey! Give over!' he said, wading through a swamp of wool.

Wallace opened the door, and to his great surprise he found Wendolene standing there. For a moment he was lost for words and all he could do was grin.

'I'm sorry about this,' said Wendolene.

'About what?' asked Wallace, puzzled.

'Oh, nothing – just stay away from me and my shop and my silly windows!' sobbed Wendolene, turning and walking away.

'But... well... I mean,' stammered Wallace, completely lost for words.

'Forget me,' wailed Wendolene, 'I'm no good for you... and I'm so sorry about Gromit.'

Wallace watched her go, surrounded by the sheep. 'Bah,' he said, and closed the door.

As the days plodded by the news got worse and worse. Headline followed headline:

SHEEP DOG TRIAL CONTINUES

GROMIT BIT ME, SAYS SHEPHERD

GROMIT FOUND GUILTY

And finally: **GROMIT GETS LIFE**.

The sheep were sad, Wallace was depressed, and now that Gromit was gone for ever, he felt as if there was no one who really cared about him at all.

'Oh, Gromit,' moaned Wallace, shaking his head.

In his prison cell Gromit had little to do all day but read. He was half way through Dogstoyevsky's *Crime and Punishment*, when the arrival of a surprise package broke his routine. Opening it he found it to be a five-thousand piece jigsaw puzzle of a flock of sheep. Gromit could have cried. What a cruel joke!

Later that night, boredom forced him to start doing the puzzle. That was when he found the hidden message it contained, saying: FRIDAY NIGHT, 8.00 PM, BE READY – A FRIEND.

Gromit quickly glanced at his calendar. Today was Friday; he checked his alarm clock – it was 8.00 pm! Then he heard a scuffling noise at his window. Looking up, he saw Shaun! And what's more, Shaun had an electric saw with him and was setting about cutting through the bars in the cell window.

Sparks flew as if it was Guy Fawkes Night as Shaun zipped through first one, then the second bar. When he'd finished Gromit stood on his chair and poked his head out of the window. He couldn't believe what he saw. Shaun was balancing at the top of a wobbly column of sheep, that was in turn perched on Wallace's shoulders. As Gromit climbed out, Wallace slipped and lost his footing. Landing flat on his back, Wallace watched as Gromit and the sheep came hurtling towards him. But their mission had been accomplished. Gromit was free!

Later that night, Wallace and Gromit, and their trusty motorbike were hiding behind a stone wall somewhere in the depths of the country.

'I suppose you'll have to skip the country now, or you'll be hunted down like a dog,' said Wallace, shaking his head.

Before Wallace could say any more, there was the sound of splintering wood. Preston's lorry smashed through the gate into the field and screeched to a halt in front of Wallace's flock of sheep. In an effort to see what was going on, the two friends disguised themselves as a scarecrow and got on their motorbike, still hidden behind the wall.

'Stop it, Preston!' they heard Wendolene say. 'I want no more of this rustling.'

Preston growled in reply, but the last thing he sounded like was a dog.

Wallace and Gromit sat still on the motorbike, hardly daring to breathe, watching as Wendolene and the sheep backed away from the advancing Preston.

'Daddy didn't create you for this!' she said. 'You're supposed to *protect* me!' Preston shoved her up the ramp into the back of the lorry with the rest of the flock, then closed the tailgate.

'Let me out!' shouted Wendolene. 'You're not going to turn me into dog meat!'

'Dog meat?' exclaimed Wallace in amazement as Preston started up the lorry. 'Don't worry Wendolene – everything's under control!' called Wallace optimistically as the lorry roared out of the field!

Quickly removing their scarecrow disguise, Wallace and Gromit sped off after the lorry, trying desperately to reach Wendolene. But out on the open road they somehow lost sight of the lorry. As they shot past a disused barn, the lorry emerged and chased after them. Preston picked up speed, trying to run them off the road! But Wallace and Gromit had a trick up their sleeves. Fitting the ladder into his sidecar Gromit climbed to the top of it, grabbed hold of some wires and performed an incredible stunt. To Preston's utter amazement the motorbike sailed over his lorry and landed safely behind him!

Wallace and Gromit were feeling rather pleased with themselves until a bolt holding the sidecar to the bike came loose. Gromit and the sidecar went sailing off down a side road and hurtled though a wooden barrier. At the last minute he saw it said:

DANGER: 2,000 FOOT DROP!

Gromit went into a nose-dive, staring at the ground as it flew up at an alarming rate. Things started to look bad for him. But Gromit was sitting in no ordinary sidecar: this one had been built by Wallace. He calmly pushed a button in front of him and instantly, as if by magic, a propeller, wings and a tail shot out of cunningly-concealed compartments around the sidecar and it converted into a plane. The propeller whirled into life and at the very last moment, Gromit pulled the plane up out of its death-dive.

Meanwhile, Wallace was up to some dare-devil acrobatics of his own.

'Don't worry, Wendolene!' he called out, crawling along the ladder he had now manoeuvred so that it rested between the bike and the lorry. 'I'm on my way!'

Wallace undid the tailgate and it slammed down. He almost lost his grip but just managed to hold on, creating a human bridge from the lorry to his bike. Shaun was the first one out, hopping over Wallace's back, and he was soon followed by the rest of the flock.

'Hey, steady on. Ouch!' yelled Wallace, his nose nearly touching the road. 'Single file! Single file, I said!'

Preston had been concentrating so hard on his driving that he hadn't had time to check his rear-view mirror. When he did, he was shocked by what he saw. Behind him, a great big woolly triangle of sheep was balanced precariously on top of Wallace's bike, with Wallace up in the top row! Preston had no idea how the stupid animals had managed to escape, but the evidence was right there behind him. He could see the lamb in the knitted jumper clinging grimly to the handlebars, steering what looked like the world's weirdest motorcycle display team but there was no sign of Wendolene. Preston realised she hadn't yet escaped.

As he approached a bridge, Preston thought the display team would be for it, for tunnels, as even sheep know, are by no means triangular. But he was wrong. The sheep immediately changed formation into an arch and just made it through to the other side. But before they could reorganise themselves, Preston played his trump card. Stamping on the brakes, he felt the bike hit the tailgate and heard the muffled thump of a flock of

High above the road, Gromit could see exactly what was going on and he knew just what to do. Swiftly mixing up a nice, thick batch of porridge, he loaded the cannon and prepared to do battle. The first thing Preston knew – PHFUUUDDD! – a great dollop of porridge splatted his wing mirror and, looking out of the window, he saw Gromit flying low beside the lorry. Then – PHFUUUUDDD-DE-DUD-DUD-DUD! – more porridge thudded against the side of the lorry. But Preston managed to get his window shut before Gromit could fire any more. Gromit was about to fire again when he saw he was flying straight at the clock tower outside Wendolene's shop. Hauling back on the controls, he climbed up into the night sky, and when he looked back down, the lorry was nowhere to be seen.

Unseen by Gromit, Preston had driven though a hidden door and was now in a huge factory behind the wool shop. Transferring Wallace, Wendolene and the sheep to a wagon, he went over to a control console and steered them towards a big machine.

'Where'd you get that from?' said Wallace, amazed to see an exact copy of his Knit-o-matic. 'That's my machine – I've got a patent pending on that!'

But before he could say another word, Preston pressed a button and the wagon tipped everyone into the washer. Everyone, that is, except Shaun...

Fascinated by the workings of his brand new machine, Preston failed to notice the escapee. While he twiddled knobs on the control console, Shaun tip-toed over to a panel of master switches. He was about to do something (he wasn't sure what) when he heard Wendolene scream and he saw that Preston had turned on a suction tube and was about to suck everyone into the dryer.

'Help, Shaun!' yelled Wendolene. 'Do something!'

And so Shaun did. He flicked switch after switch on the panel, but nothing happened. Shaun was a worried lamb. He was running out of switches to flick.

High up in the sky, Gromit was beginning to get worried as well – where could Wallace and the rest of them be? And then a sign on a tall chimney suddenly lit up, illuminating the night sky. It said PRESTON'S DOG FOOD...

Gromit rolled the plane and made a dive for the factory, tearing off his flying helmet and ducking down as the plane levelled out and bored straight through the wooden factory doors. It flew on and bored through a second metal door, then flew on again and began chewing through a brick wall. The engine whined, dust billowed everywhere and the wings snapped off, but at last Gromit was through and making straight for Preston.

'Attaboy, Gromit!' yelled Wallace, as his faithful dog began firing rounds of porridge. Preston staggered back, but recovered in time to grab the propeller, sending the plane into a spin, flinging Gromit up into the roof.

It took Preston a moment to regain his balance, which was just enough time for Shaun to reposition the suction tube and **THWIIIPP!** the horrible hound was sucked up into the dryer. Then the Knit-o-matic quickly whipped Preston into its shearing section. Seeing what had happened, Gromit snatched a rope tied to a blacksmith's anvil and jumped down. The heavy lump of iron counterbalanced his weight and stopped him right by the Knit-o-matic's control panel. Winking at Shaun, Gromit was able to turn the dial from *Light Shave* to *Close Shave* before the anvil hauled him up to the roof again. 'Well done, Gromit,' grinned Wallace, 'that'll teach him!'

But something was going very wrong with the Knit-o-matic. From inside the machine came a series of loud thumps, bangs and gruesome snarls, and then alarming bulges started to appear in its metal casing.

Wallace, Wendolene and the sheep watched in horror as the strain and stress meters both went into the red zone and the cutter blades reappeared all bent and twisted. 'He's malfunctioning!' said Wendolene.

'Mal what?' asked a confused Wallace, as the machine's needles started knitting.

'Malfunctioning... Preston's a cyberdog,' explained Wendolene.

'Cyber what?' frowned Wallace, watching a jumper begin to appear.

'A robot,' said Wendolene. 'Daddy created him to do good, but he's turned evil.'

At that very moment a steel paw punched a hole in the Knit-o-matic's casing and reached round to open a door. Out strode Preston – the real, metallic Preston, now stripped of his outer shell.

No one moved. They didn't dare. And then Preston jerked forward menacingly, stretching out to grab Shaun and crush him in his arms. But before he could get the little lamb, Gromit plummeted from the ceiling, and picked Shaun up, before the anvil wooshed them both safely out of Preston's reach. Frustrated, Preston turned and roared at the others.

The cyberdog was enraged. 'Eeeek!' squeaked Wallace and Wendolene, as he clanked towards them.

But the Knit-o-matic, calmly clicking through its program, suddenly went into delivery mode and plonked the jumper it had just completed over Preston's head. Momentarily blinded, the cyberdog accidentally knocked a lever that proceeded to activate the platform on which they were all standing, which slowly began to lift them up level with a moving conveyer belt. As the platform was raised, Wallace spotted a contraption with a huge set of spiked rollers. A label said PRESTON'S MUTTON-O-MATIC and behind it was a canning machine.

'Now *that's* clever!' said Wallace.

High up in the roof Gromit let out a piercing whistle to attract Wallace's attention and then swung down on his rope. Preston, still unable to see what was going on through the double-knit dog-hair jumper, had no idea what hit him when Gromit pushed him on to the conveyer belt. Horrified, Wallace saw Gromit himself fall on to the belt as Preston finally tore the jumper off his head.

'Do something, Wallace!' screamed Wendolene, and he did; leaping over to the control console he tried to stop the Mutton-o-matic. Unfortunately, all he succeeded in doing was to make the belt go even faster!

Gromit was running quicker than he ever had – not only did he have a murderous robot on his tail, but a mincing machine was trying to get him as well! Driven by desperation, Wallace pushed every lever he could see at once... and sent the platform they were all standing on tipping up at one end.

Wallace, Wendolene and the sheep all fell on to the conveyer belt, joining Gromit and Preston in a sprint for their lives as the rollers whirled faster and faster, their spikes glinting.

Out of the corner of her eye, Wendolene saw a strange object hurtling towards them out of the gloom. It was Shaun, clinging to the anvil!

'Duck!' she yelled.

'Where?' panted Wallace, confused, and then he too saw Shaun and swiftly dodged out of the way.

'Baaaaa-aaahhh!' bleated Shaun swishing over everyone's head, only just missing Gromit as he swung at Preston. The cyberdog didn't have a chance and Shaun thundered into him with a resounding **CLANG-G-G!**

The force of the collision knocked Preston off his balance and pushed him into the Mutton-o-matic's hungry teeth.

There followed a series of ghastly crunching, tearing, gobbling noises and all of a sudden the Mutton-o-matic ground to a halt. Wallace, Wendolene, Gromit and the sheep were still running for all they were worth when the conveyor belt stopped moving. From being inches from the jaws of death, they suddenly found themselves in a large heap of arms, legs and wool.

'By 'eck!' said Wallace. 'I thought we were all for the can then!'

Silence fell over the factory while everyone tried to get untangled. They could hardly believe their luck – they were alive! Preston had been foiled and his evil plan to turn them all into dog food had completely misfired. The silence was broken as the Mutton-o-matic slowly began to start working once more, its complex gears completing the job it had been designed to do. The canning production line began to move, tins shuffling underneath a chute that filled each one up to the top with what had so recently been a rather nasty robot dog.

Preston had gone to pieces.

Completely.

A few days later, Number 62's doorbell rang and Wallace went to see who was there. Opening the door he smiled – it was Wendolene!

'I couldn't pass by without saying thank you,' she said. Wendolene pressed a button on the remote control in her hand, and the redesigned mechanical mutt came into view, carrying a newspaper in his mouth. 'He's just like he used to be.'

'Oh, don't mention it,' grinned Wallace, reaching down to take the paper. 'Thanks, pooch... Won't you come in? We were just about to have some cheese'.

'Oh, no, not cheese,' frowned Wendolene, 'sorry, it brings me out in a rash – can't stand the stuff!'

'Not even Wensleydale?' asked Wallace.

'Got to be on our way. Come on, Preston,' stammered Wendolene, a tear in her eye. 'Goodbye, chuck.'

Wallace closed the door. 'What's wrong with Wensleydale?' he muttered, sitting down in his armchair.

Gromit looked up from the paper. The headline read GROMIT EXONERATED, as he'd been cleared of any blame for the sheep rustling and murders. He looked at Wallace.

'Talking of cheese,' said Wallace, brightening up considerably, 'there'll be all the more for us, and not a sheep to worry about!'

Reaching over to the table, he lifted the cover off the cheese dish to discover Shaun hiding underneath it – and he'd eaten all the Wensleydale!

'Aww!' exclaimed Wallace angrily. 'Get off me cheese! Get off! Gromit! Gromit – go for him!'

Gromit raised his eyebrows and sighed. Everything, he thought to himself, was as back to normal as it could possibly be.

'BAAH!'

First published in 1996 by BBC Children's Books
a division of BBC Worldwide Publishing Ltd
Woodlands, 80 Wood Lane, London W12 0TT

ISBN 0 563 40406 X
Printed by Cambus Litho, East Kilbride
Bound by Hunter & Foulis Ltd, Edinburgh
Cover printed by Clays Ltd, St Ives plc
Colour separations by DOT Gradations, Chelmsford